YOUR DAD'S A MONKEY

By evening, Robert, George and Albinia had stretched out the hammocks and hauled up the bath, and everything they had brought with them was up the tree. Then, after supper, George and Albinia announced that it was Robert's bedtime.

"It's only seven-thirty," protested Robert, "and I want to watch T.V. It's my programme."

"T.V.!" George was appalled. "What are you talking about? We don't need T.V. any more. We are OUTDOORS! Above us, the velvet sky, around us the sleeping birds, and the little night animals skipping from their homes to start their day."

Robert was deeply embarrassed to hear his father talking like this but Albinia seemed to like it. "That's beautiful, George," she whispered and took hold of his father's arm in a way that made Robert feel like being sick.

"Yuk!" he said very loudly.

His parents looked at him. "Go to bed. Now!"

**Also by the same author,
and available in Knight Books:**

The Wrestling Princess and Other Stories
Oskar and the Ice-Pick

Your Dad's a Monkey

JUDY CORBALIS

Illustrated by Tony Ross

KNIGHT BOOKS
Hodder and Stoughton

For Toby, with love

Text copyright © 1989 by Judy Corbalis

Illustrations copyright © 1989 by Tony Ross

First published in Great Britain in 1989 by André Deutsch Limited

Knight edition published 1991

British Library C.I.P.

Corbalis, Judy
  Your dad's a monkey.
  I. Title
  823'914 [J]

ISBN 0 340 53128 2

Printed and bound in Great Britain for Hodder and Stoughton Children's Books, a division of Hodder and Stoughton Ltd., Mill Road, Dunton Green, Sevenoaks, Kent TN13 2YA. (Editorial Office: 47 Bedford Square, London WC1B 3DP) by Cox & Wyman Ltd., Reading.

1

Robert was a very ordinary boy. He lived with his mother and father in a perfectly ordinary house in an ordinary street opposite the park. Every morning his father put on his hat, picked up his umbrella from the hall, and went off to work. His mother put on an apron, got out the vacuum cleaner and did the housework. And Robert put on his anorak, picked up his lunchbox and went off to school.

In the afternoon when he got home, his mother would open the door and say, "Hullo, dear. Did you have a nice day?" Then they would have tea and sometimes go shopping together and later, when his father came back from work, they would all have supper and talk a bit, then Robert would go to bed. Robert liked his life exactly the way it was.

But one day when he got home from school, his *father* opened the door and said, "You're home early, Robert."

"I always get home now," said Robert. "You're the one that's early."

"Today is a very important day," said his father. "It's Day One. This family has become stale and boring. From today things are going to be different. We

must get out of the rut we've sunk into."

Robert came inside. "I like being in a rut," he said. "It's comfortable."

"It's not good for you," said his father. "No challenge. No stimulation. It's unhealthy."

"I'm quite healthy," said Robert.

"So from now on," went on his father, taking no notice, "we are making *changes*."

An uneasy feeling came over Robert but he decided to ignore it.

At breakfast next morning, Robert's father said, "We shall start our new exciting life straight away. From now on, you are to call us Albinia and George, not Mum and Dad."

"I *like* calling you Mum and Dad," protested Robert. "All the other kids call their parents that!"

"Exactly," said his father. "Too ordinary."

"George is old-fashioned," said Robert. "I'd feel silly calling you that."

"George is a very good name," snapped his father. "And that's no way to speak to your father."

"You just said we should have equality," said Robert.

"Don't be cheeky," said George. "You're so argumentative, Robert."

"I am not!" said Robert indignantly.

"There you go again," sighed his father. "Most boys would be pleased to be allowed to call their parents by their names."

"No one else does," protested Robert.

"Be the first," said George. "Be a leader."

3

"I am a leader," said Robert. "I'm captain of the football team."

"Football!" said George. "What's football got to do with it? From now on, we are George and Albinia and that's that. No more argument."

"That's not equality," said Robert. "Equality's everyone having a say."

"Will you be quiet?" cried George. "Or do you want a clip round the ear?"

Robert glowered at his father. "Equality!" he snorted under his breath. "Huh!"

They finished breakfast in silence, then Robert watched George put on his hat and pick up his umbrella and Albinia put on her apron and get out the vacuum cleaner, and he went off to school feeling a bit more worried than he had yesterday.

And the next morning, after breakfast, *Albinia* put on the bowler hat, kissed George and Robert and went off to the office, George put on the apron and started on the housework and Robert crept off to school feeling very worried indeed.

Then, the morning after that, as Albinia was putting on the hat, George said, "Living in an ordinary house is not what this family needs. Yesterday, as I was peeling the potatoes, I had an absolutely original idea. We shall move out of our house and live in a treehouse in the park."

"There isn't a treehouse in the park," said Robert.

"So we shall build one," said George.

"Build one!" said Robert. "But, Dad . . ."

"Close your mouth," said George. "I can see the toast on your tonsils. It's no use arguing. My mind is made up. We shall start tomorrow."

And they did.

2

"We won't need any furniture," said Albinia. "Well, hardly any. Just a few cushions and a low table and a washing up bowl. And a bath of course."

Robert was indignant. "What about my BED?"

"We'll sleep on the floor," said George. "Much healthier."

"We haven't *got* a floor yet," said Robert.

So Albinia went out and bought three hammocks – one for them, one for Robert and one for the clothing. She also bought a big beach umbrella.

"In case it rains," she explained.

Robert felt very unhappy about leaving his nice ordinary waterproof house, and after he'd put some of his best things into a suitcase, he took his pocket money and went off gloomily to the hardware shop round the corner.

When he got back, George and Albinia were putting things in a pile in the hall. Robert brought his suitcase downstairs.

"What's in it?" asked George.

"Meccano," said Robert. "And Lego, and my model planes and some books and my Action Man and my radio-car and my walkie . . ."

"Robert," said George, "we are moving to live up a tree. We are pioneers – unusual, different, trailblazers. You are *not* taking all that rubbish with you."

"It's *not* rubbish," cried Robert. "It's my luggage."

"I don't think you realize," said George more kindly, "that from now on you won't need all that. Who needs books when you can write your own poetry?

Who needs Meccano when you can build your own models from the trees?"

"I do," said Robert. "I don't want to live up a tree and I hate woodwork."

"When I was your age . . ." began George.

"Dear," said Albinia hastily, "I do think we should get started." George threw Robert a frosty look and went off to collect some blankets.

"Mum," said Robert.

"Albinia, dear."

Robert sighed. "Albinia. *Please* can't you get him to stop it?"

"But this will be the adventure of a lifetime."

"Can't he go and live in the tree on his own? You and I could stay here by ourselves."

Albinia shot Robert a reproachful look. "I don't think that's very nice," she said. "Of course I want to live up a tree. It'll be terribly exciting. And you certainly can't stay here on your own so you'll just have to make the best of it."

"I'd like to murder them," thought Robert. "What'll the others say to me at school?"

And aloud he said, "I don't *want* to live up a tree."

"We heard you the first time," said George coming back downstairs. "That's just too bad. Now start helping Albinia and me to carry these things over to our new home."

8

3

In two hours they had all their things under the largest tree in the park and it was lunchtime. Albinia opened the sardines and the cake tin, and they sat under their new home to eat. During the meal George and Albinia decided they should start building on the fourth branch from the ground.

"Why?" asked Robert.

"Because it's the longest," explained George.

"And the prettiest," added Albinia.

"There's a great big crack in it," said Robert. "The one above's better."

So the fifth branch from the ground became their new home.

All afternoon they hung clothing and towels from the tree, rigged up a rope ladder and nailed up a small wooden platform for the tin bath.

"How do we fill it?" asked Robert.

"With a hose, of course," said George. "I'm going to run one from that park tap over there."

"That's only a cold water tap," said Robert.

"We'll have cold water baths," said George. "It's much healthier, and besides, living outdoors all the time, we won't feel the cold."

Robert was outraged. "I'm going to go back and take baths in the old house," he announced loudly.

"You can't, dear," said Albinia. "I've switched the boiler off."

Robert kicked viciously at a tin can that was lying nearby.

"Don't do that," said Albinia. "Put it in the rubbish bin."

"I didn't drop it," said Robert.

"Don't answer back," said George. "Do as you're told."

George was not feeling well. He was not used to sardines and cake for lunch and his stomach hurt. He wished Albinia had been able to make a healthy salad but she'd been too busy.

"Get along now, Robert," he said crossly. "Hurry up."

Robert pulled a face behind George's back. "He's mad," he muttered to himself as he kicked the can towards the bin. "They're both mad. My parents have gone bonkers."

"Pick up that can this minute!" boomed a loud voice. Robert looked up, startled. The park-keeper was striding towards him.

"I'm kicking it over to the litter bin," he explained. "It's not my can either. Someone else dropped it."

"Oh yes," said the park-keeper. "And you're just kicking it along out of the goodness of your heart."

11

"That's right," said Robert.

"Don't you give me lip," said the keeper threateningly. "I've got enough on my plate with that lot over there." And he pointed at George and Albinia's tree.

"Littering up the park with buckets and hammocks and whatnot. It's a disgrace. Nailed up a platform, they have. Look at it! A bath up a tree! I ask you! They must be raving mad."

Robert put the can in the rubbish bin.

"They'll be taking it down as soon as I get hold of them," went on the park-keeper, straightening his jacket and cap.

Robert brightened. "Will they?"

"They certainly will," promised the keeper. "The cheek of it. Moving in to live in one of my trees."

"What if they won't go?" asked Robert.

"Have to, won't they?" said the park-keeper. "It's against regulations.

Robert thought quickly. "I have to be off now," he said. "'Bye."

"'Bye," said the keeper. "Watch your litter."

Robert slipped off behind some bushes where he could watch what was going on without being seen.

The park-keeper strode up to the tree. "Hi! You there!"

George's face appeared through the leaves. "Yes?"

"What do you mean by squatting up my tree? You're breaking regulations, you are," called the park-keeper.

"Nonsense!" said George. "This is a free country and I can live wherever I choose."

"Not in my park, you can't," shouted the park-keeper. "You leave right now and take all that rubbish with you."

"That 'rubbish' is my furniture," said George, "and I have no intention of moving any of it. Or of leaving my new home."

"You come on down here this minute," bellowed the keeper. "I'm getting the law on you."

George was unmoved.

"Did you hear me?" yelled the keeper.

"My good man," said George kindly, "I have no idea why you should feel so upset."

"No idea!" spluttered the keeper. "I like that! Living up one of my trees like some orang-utan and he says he's got no idea why I should feel upset. It's against the law, what you're doing!"

"It most certainly is not," said George. "I've checked the byelaws thoroughly and I'm perfectly within my legal rights to live up any tree I choose."

"You've got to be crazy to choose to live up a tree in the first place," shouted the park-keeper. "A lunatic! That's what you are! Deranged!"

George looked pityingly down at him. "We are pioneers of the New Age life. Living back to Nature side by side with Art. In a very short time every tree in this park will be colonized by families who have followed our lead."

Albinia poked her head through the leaves.

"I'm amazed they let him loose," said the keeper. "Are you his minder, then?"

Albinia looked upset.

"You take him off out of here and all his hammocks and buckets and whatnots," said the keeper. "Right away. And that's an order!" And he strode furiously away, muttering.

Behind the bushes, Robert grinned to himself.

"What a horrible man," said Albinia.

"We have to expect it, I'm afraid," said George. "The man's a Philistine. No feeling for the Real Life at all."

"Can he force us to leave?" asked Albinia.

"Not at all," said George. "There's nothing in the byelaws to stop us. We're perfectly legally entitled to be here. This is my new home and here I intend to stay."

Behind the bushes, Robert's heart sank.

4

By evening, Robert, George and Albinia had stretched out the hammocks and hauled up the bath, and everything they had brought with them was up the tree. Robert had hung a bucket on the end of a long rope so they could pull up their milk and letters. Supper had been fish and chips which had made him feel better but had upset George even more.

"We're supposed to be *healthy* and living back to Nature," he complained.

"I can't make supper out of nothing," said Albinia. "Unless you want to eat grass."

Then, after supper, George and Albinia announced that it was Robert's bedtime.

"It's only seven-thirty," protested Robert. "My bedtime's eight-thirty."

"Not any more," said Albinia. "Not now we're living out of doors."

"You'll be up with the sun at dawn," said George. "Just like the rest of Nature's creatures."

"But I want to watch T.V. It's my programme," wailed Robert.

"T.V!" George was appalled. "What are you talking

about? We don't need T.V. any more. We are OUT-
DOORS! Above us, the velvet sky, around us the
sleeping birds, and the little night animals skipping
from their homes to start their day."

Robert was deeply embarrassed to hear his father
talking like this but Albinia seemed to like it. "That's
beautiful, George," she whispered and took hold of
his father's arm in a way that made Robert feel like
being sick.

"Yuk!" he said very loudly.

His parents looked at him. "Go to bed. Now!"
ordered George and Robert slunk off to his hammock
feeling miserable and wronged. He lay in the dark for
what seemed like a very long time. It was chilly and
rather damp and there was a cold draught round his
ears. The hammock wasn't very comfortable either
and when he turned over there wasn't much room
at the edges.

Robert thought about his old bed that he had
been sleeping in just yesterday. It was warm and
comfortable. And the room was nice, too. He had
posters on the walls and models on his bookshelf
and his computer was . . .

His thoughts were interrupted by the sounds of
George and Albinia going to bed. He heard them
getting into their hammock.

"Tomorrow," said George, "we begin to build
our new home."

"Isn't that exciting?" said Albinia.

"No!" called Robert from his hammock. "I liked the old home best."

Albinia and George ignored this. George inhaled deeply. "Ah!" he breathed, "smell those glorious leaves."

"A little one dropped gently on my face," murmured Albinia.

"That's rain," said Robert. "It's just started."

"RAIN!!" cried his parents sitting bolt upright. Zip! Snap! Twist! Over and over went their ham-

mock, tangling the two of them tightly in its strings.

Robert heaved a sigh. He carefully rolled out of his own hammock, undid his emergency kit and pulled out a large square of plastic. Then he climbed up several branches higher and tied each end of the plastic securely to the branches of the tree. George and Albinia were struggling to untangle themselves but they were so knotted up, it was impossible. Robert pushed aside the rope ladder, slid down the trunk to the next branch, crawled along it till he was below their hammock, then gave it an enormous shove and spun them back in the opposite direction. They both flew out of the hammock, dropped through the branches and bumped onto the ground.

"Ow!" screeched George. Albinia felt herself for broken bones.

"Are you all right?" cried George.

"I think so," said Albinia. "But I'm a bit sore. Are you hurt?"

"I've wrenched my arm," said George, annoyed. "That damned hammock. I'm covered in muck and rubbish."

From above them they heard Robert's voice floating down. "It's all right," he said. "It's just good, natural earth."

And, as he heard them scrambling up the trunk, he climbed back into his own hammock, put his pillow over his head and went to sleep.

5

Next day was Sunday. George and Albinia were still asleep when Robert woke up. For a minute he couldn't think where he was, then he remembered and his heart sank. He peered through the branches. It had stopped raining but was still very muddy underfoot. He got out of the hammock carefully, stood in the bath and put his clothes on. Then he quickly opened the cake tin, fished out the last piece of cake and drank the rest of the milk. The sun was quite high in the sky although it wasn't very bright and there seemed to be rather a lot of people wandering and strolling in the park already. What if someone recognized him? What was he going to tell them at school?

Well, today was Sunday so he had a whole day to think about it! Sunday! Robert started. That was the day Grandmother Williams came to lunch. Every Sunday she arrived at eleven ready to eat at midday. He had a feeling she wouldn't be too pleased with sardines for lunch and he'd eaten all the cake. Maybe she wouldn't come now they were living up the tree. She mightn't know where to find them.

He looked over towards the old house and saw

her standing at the gate talking to Mr Dix, their next-door neighbour. Mr Dix was pointing at the tree. Even from this distance, Grandmother Williams didn't look too pleased. Robert climbed up two more branches to get a better view. Grandmother Williams came marching across the park clutching her umbrella and her carpet bag. He decided to stay where he was.

She appeared under the tree. "George!" she shouted.

There was silence, then from the fifth branch came the sound of a groan. Robert's father peered through the branches. Mud and bits of leaf and twig were still stuck to his hair.

"Come down here AT ONCE!" thundered Grand-

mother Williams.

Albinia and George scrambled down. They looked dreadfully muddy and tired. Grandmother Williams was short and fat and furious: she brandished her umbrella angrily at George. "What is the meaning of this?" she demanded. "I've never *heard* such nonsense and goings-on in my life. A grown-up man and his wife and child living up a tree like apes! I'm not having it! I refuse to visit my only daughter's family up a tree."

"We're living back to Nature," explained George.

"Back to Nature!" Grandmother Williams was scornful. "Back to front, more like. I always thought you had your head on backwards, George Parker, and now I know for sure."

Albinia put a timid hand on her mother's sleeve. "Mother," she said gently.

Robert poked his head out of the branches. "Ivy," he said. "You have to call her 'Ivy' now. You're not allowed to call her Mother any more. George said."

"I'll 'Ivy' you," said his grandmother. "Just get yourself down here *this minute*, young man."

Robert slid hastily down the trunk tearing his trousers on the way.

"I do *not* intend to have Sunday lunch with my only daughter's family in a public park," said Grandmother Williams. "Robert, you're a very naughty boy. You must have had a hand in this. Fancy persuading your family to live up a tree." She turned to George and Albinia. "You should have known better. I'm astounded at you."

"Me!" said Robert indignantly. "*I* don't want to live up a tree. It wasn't *my* idea."

"It was mine," said George. "This family was boring and uninteresting. It was time for a change."

"When this family decides to come to its senses and live in a house again, let me know," snapped Grandmother Williams. "In the meantime, I shall *not* be visiting you." She glowered at George and Albinia. "You're utterly irresponsible, allowing Robert to persuade you into this," she said crossly, and before they had time to answer, she turned and strode away out of the park.

6

Albinia was upset. "I've never seen Mother like that," she said.

"You have to call her Ivy," said Robert.

"Be quiet, Robert," said George.

"But you said . . ." began Robert.

"I *know* what I said," said George crabbily. "Just *shut up* for a minute."

He put his arm round Albinia. "She'll get used to the idea," he said. "She'll be proud to be related to us when she sees how original and interesting we are."

"We'd better get started then," said Robert.

George reached out to clip Robert's ear but Robert was too quick for him. Albinia continued to look doubtful.

"Let's have a cup of tea," suggested George.

"There's no milk," said Robert.

"It's all right," said Albinia. "I left a note for the milkman and I can see the milk float over there now."

"Did you ask him to deliver it to the tree?" said George.

"Of course," said Albinia and they climbed back up

the trunk to put the water on to boil on the camping stove.

"Hullo!" shouted a voice from below. There stood the milkman holding the note and peering up into the branches.

"Over here!" shouted George. "Same as usual. Three pints of milk, two yoghurts and an orange juice, please."

"Sorry, Guv," said the milkman, "can't do it. No rules about having to deliver up trees, I'm afraid."

"But it's simple," explained Albinia. "You just put the order into that bucket there and we pull up the rope."

"Too dangerous," said the milkman. "S'pose a bottle fell out and smashed on someone's head. What then?"

"We'll be careful," said Albinia.

"Can't do it, love," said the milkman. "The company'd hold me responsible if anything happened. You'll have to buy it at the corner shop. Sorry." And he went away whistling.

"Just pop down to the shop and get two pints, will you," said George to Robert.

"I don't want to," said Robert.

"The exercise is good for you," said George.

"Why don't *you* go?" asked Robert.

"Don't be rude," said George. "And arrange for the shop to deliver a newspaper as well, please."

"I'm not rude," said Robert. "I just don't want to go." But he slid down the trunk and stumped off to the shop.

" 'Morning, Robert," said the shopman.

" 'Morning," mumbled Robert. "Three pints of milk, please."

"Here you are," said the shopman, putting them on the counter.

"And I've come about the paper," went on Robert.

"Take it with you," said the shopman. "Delivery girl's late this morning."

"It's about the delivery," said Robert, going pink. "George, I mean, my dad, I mean, he . . ."

"Yes," said the shopman. "What is it?"

"We've moved," said Robert desperately. "So we need the paper at our new place."

The door at the back of the shop opened and a girl of Robert's age appeared in the doorway. "Can I have a Mars bar, Dad?" She noticed Robert. "Hi, Robert!"

Robert went bright red.

"Robert's moved," said her father. "Didn't know your parents were planning a change of house. Your mother was in here last week but she never mentioned it."

"We just moved yesterday," said Robert. "We went suddenly."

"What's the new address, then," said the shopman. "I'll put it in the delivery book."

He lifted down a big black book from the shelf. Robert went an even brighter red. "It's . . . it's . . . er . . ."

A woman came into the shop behind him.

"Hurry up, now," said the shopman. "I haven't got all day."

"It's . . . that is . . . I mean . . . we've moved to live up a tree," blurted out Robert. "And George, I mean Dad, he . . . he . . . he wants you to deliver our paper up the tree from now on. It's the big one with the platform and there's a bucket on a rope underneath to put the paper in."

The girl began to giggle.

"Deliver your paper up a tree!" said the shopman. "Are you trying to be smart with me, Robert?"

"No," said Robert, looking at his feet. "I'm not. Honestly. It's true. We *do* live up a tree now."

"Stop all that nonsense this minute," said the shopman angrily. "Take your milk and get along."

Robert raced out of the shop, red and angry.

"You can go yourself and explain," he shouted as he climbed up the ladder. "I'm not going again. *And* his girl's in my class at school. She'll tell everyone tomorrow."

"They'll all think you're very lucky," soothed Albinia.

"Huh!" said Robert. "That's all you know."

7

Next morning Robert got himself ready for school. It was difficult washing and dressing up a tree but yesterday, after Grandmother Williams had gone, he and George and Albinia had built the main platform of their house and Robert had tied another piece of plastic securely above it to keep the rain out. It was cold in amongst the leaves. Robert shivered. He wasn't looking forward to going to school. Everyone would have heard about his new home by now. Cindy from the corner shop would've told all her friends. "I'll just have to pretend I like it," he decided.

He poured milk on some cornflakes, added a banana, ate them, then started down the trunk with his school things. Albinia had given him some money to buy his lunch. "Just this once," she'd said.

His parents seemed to be still asleep in their hammock. "Lazy things," thought Robert.

Albinia opened her eyes. "Goodbye, dear!" she called. Robert pretended not to hear her.

"Robert," said George, yawning, "your mother's speaking to you."

"She's going to be late for work," muttered Robert.

"Work!" said George. "She's not going to *work* again. And neither am I. We gave all that up when we left that boring life we had before."

Robert brightened. He began climbing back up the trunk. "So I don't have to go to school, either."

"Of course you do," said George and Albinia together.

"Why?" demanded Robert. "*You* aren't going to work. Why should I have to go to school?"

"School's quite different from work," explained Albinia.

"I don't see why," said Robert. "We work really hard at my school."

"And besides," said George, "*we* are grown up. *You* are still a child. I had to go to school and so did Albinia. And so do you."

"That's not equality!" cried Robert.

"Stop raving on about equality," said George. "It's far too early in the morning."

"You said we were going to have equality," bellowed Robert. "You said . . ."

"For goodness sake, don't be so literal-minded," said George, rolling over in the hammock.

"Well, I'm not going to school," said Robert. "And that's all there is to it."

George sat up carefully in his hammock. "You're going to school right now, THIS MINUTE," he said meaningly. "Unless you want me to help you on your way."

Robert glowered at his father. "Huh!" he snorted and slid down the trunk tearing his socks on purpose on the way down.

He had just set off across the park when a thought struck him. "If you don't go to work, how will you get money?" he called up into the branches.

George's head protruded amongst the leaves. "Money!" he said disdainfully. "We don't need *money*. Albinia is going to catch fish and I am going to go birdwatching."

Robert was puzzled. "I don't see how birdwatching's going to help us get food."

"I'm going to watch pigeons and catch them for our supper," said George. "Now off you go to school." And he withdrew his head.

Robert stamped angrily along the park paths. The park-keeper appeared round the corner. " 'Morning," he called.

Robert grunted.

"Not very civil this morning," remarked the park-keeper.

"You wouldn't be civil, either, if you had my life," muttered Robert but the keeper didn't hear him.

Outside the park he met the postman. "Hullo," said the postman. "You've moved."

"Huh!" said Robert.

"Can't deliver any more letters or parcels, I'm afraid," said the postman. "It's against regulations. Not up a tree. I can leave them at the old address if you want, though."

"Yes, please," said Robert.

He went on to school and his heart sank as he approached the entrance.

8

Just inside the school gates, there was a group of children clustered round waiting for him. Cindy from the corner shop whispered something to the others and they all giggled. Robert went on walking into the building, then stopped as something hit him hard on the ear. He looked down. It was a peanut! Ping! Another one caught him on the neck. Dennis Woods was laughing at him. "Breakfast time!" he shouted. Another volley of peanuts hit Robert as everyone started throwing. He stood there dazed and embarrassed and angry.

"Here," said Jason and he raced up to Robert. "A banana. Eat it up, apeman."

"Shut up!" shouted Robert.

"Cindy told us," cried Jason. "And Wayne saw your dad up there yesterday."

"Going to live up a tree!" called Dan.

Then they all started.

"Yah! Yah! should be in the Zoo."

"He's not allowed in the classroom. He has to have lessons in a cage, sir said."

"You're a liar, Dominic. That's not true."

"Peanuts!"

"Tarzan!"

"Chee! Chee! Chee! Monkey in a tree."

And Dennis said nastily, "Your dad's a monkey, that's what. He isn't a human being like our dads. He's a monkey."

"Yah! Your dad's a monkey!" everyone shouted.

"He's *not*," cried Robert. "Shut up!!"

And at that moment Jemima came in the gates.

Robert didn't like girls much, but Jemima was a bit different. She was the tallest in the class and she really was the best scorer in the football team. Sir called her 'The Amazon'. Jemima liked Robert, though he didn't know why. She'd even asked him to her birthday party. Robert had refused to go but she didn't mind. If Jemima liked you that was enough for her.

As soon as she came in the gates she saw what was going on. She went up to Jason and Dennis. "You want me to beat you up?" she asked.

"Er, no," said Jason uneasily.

"D'you?" Jemima turned to Dennis. Dennis shuffled his feet and looked at the ground.

"Lay off, then," said Jemima going into the school building.

"You can walk home with me after school if you like," she said to Robert.

"I'm all right," said Robert ungraciously.

"Are you *really* living up in a tree, then?" she asked.

Robert started to tell her to be quiet then remembered she'd done him a big favour. "Yes," he said shortly.

"It sounds great," said Jemima.

"It isn't. It's cold and there's no T.V. or anything. I haven't even got my stuff up there."

"Why're you up there, then?"

"It's my dad," explained Robert. "He likes it. He thinks it's a good idea."

"You'd better do something about it, then, hadn't you?" said Jemima.

The bell rang. Jemima was right, Robert thought. He would have to do something about it. And soon.

9

Robert had a very uncomfortable morning. Class started with Morning News. Everyone was supposed to bring a news item from the newspaper or television. There was the astronaut who'd just come back from a manned flight to Jupiter, famine relief in Central Africa, and heavy floods in India. In France, a man with a gun had taken seven children hostage and threatened to shoot them, and an Australian had invented a car that ran on water. Sir was pleased. "You've done very well," he said.

"Sir, Mr Keen, sir," said Dennis putting up his hand.

"What is it, Dennis?"

"I know some local news, sir. Something really interesting."

"Tell us then," said Mr Keen. "And quick about it. I want to get that Maths homework marked before break."

"Sir, it's interesting, sir."

"All *right*," said Mr Keen. "Get on with it."

"It's Robert, sir. His dad's taken them to live up a tree."

"His dad's a monkey, sir!" called Wayne.

Mr Keen was angry. Robert sat looking red and hot. Jemima raised her fist at Wayne behind Dominic's back.

"Be *quiet*, you lot," bellowed Mr Keen. "And, Wayne, you can stay in at break and sweep the classroom."

"But it's true, sir, it . . ."

"QUIET!" roared Mr Keen. "Get out your Maths books and not a word from any of you."

"I wish *he* was my dad," thought Robert. "I bet *he* doesn't want to live up a tree."

He didn't want to go outside at break. He was still hanging around the toilets when Dennis and Dominic came in. "You got Wayne into trouble," hissed Dennis.

"He got himself into trouble," said Robert. "And my dad's *not* a monkey."

"Chee! Chee! Chee!" said Dominic nastily. "Baboon-bum. Bet his bum's all red and blue."

The bell rang. As they went to line up, some of the kids stood scratching their armpits and making monkey noises.

"Settle *down*, Mr Keen's class," said Mrs Wright, who was on playground duty.

After playtime it was P.E. in the hall.

Robert was good at gym. He swung on the rope and climbed right to the top. "Look at the monkey climbing the ropes," hissed Andy. Robert felt hurt. Andy was supposed to be his friend. He slid down the rope. Andy moved away to stand next to Ben and Dominic.

"Keep away from the monkey," whispered Dominic. "He's got fleas – you might catch them."

"Take no notice," whispered Jemima. "You can bring your lunch home to my place if you like."

Robert ignored her.

Mr Keen divided them into teams for activities – vaulting the horse, climbing the bars, walking the upturned benches, using the ropes, and tumbling on the mats. When he blew his whistle, each team had to run to the next activity and line up there. *"Without talking,"* said Mr Keen.

Because Robert was good at gym, everyone always wanted him in their team. Usually he got picked straight away. But today it was different: nobody wanted to choose him. Dominic chose Cyril Prosser who couldn't even walk along a bench without falling off, and left Robert out. Cyril looked at Dominic in surprise.

"Robert." It was Hannah. Robert looked at Mr Keen. "I don't want to, sir. It's all girls in her team."

"It won't be all girls when you're in it, will it, Robert?" said Mr Keen.

"But, sir . . .'

"This smacks of rampant sexism," said Mr Keen with a grin. "In another few years you'll be desperate to be in their team, I can tell you."

Robert threw the teacher a sullen look.

"Quick! Get a move on! Over there with Hannah and the Beauties," said Mr Keen.

As Robert sulked his way over, he caught sight of Dominic doing a monkey imitation behind sir's back.

"Your dad's a monkey!" mouthed Dominic silently. Robert pulled a face at him but not quickly enough.

Mr Keen swung round. "What *is* all this?" he demanded.

"Sir, Dominic was making fun of him," said Hannah.

"Right," said Mr Keen. "Any trouble, one peep out of *any* of you and the lot of you stay in for the afternoon playtime. Got that?"

Everyone stood quietly. "Now get on with it. I'm going to blow the whistle and you all get started and NO MONKEY BUSINESS!"

This was too much for everyone. All of them except Robert burst into hysterical giggles. Mr Keen was livid. "I don't know what's the matter with you lot and I don't care, but you're spending afternoon playtime in the classroom with me doing extra Maths." Everyone stopped giggling. Mr Keen blew the whistle and, in dead silence, the teams started their activities.

"That was *your* fault," said Dennis viciously as they went to get changed afterwards. "If your dad didn't live up a tree like a monkey, none of us would have to stay in later."

"It was Dominic's fault," said Robert. "He was the one that was talking and being stupid. And I've got to stay in as well."

"Your dad's a monkey, a monkey, a monkey," hissed Andy.

Robert gritted his teeth as he pulled off his shirt.

10

After school, he grabbed his things as quickly as he could and set off for home. He bumped into Jemima by the gates. She walked some of the way with him. "I'm going to karate," she said. "Dan's going to meet me by the park." Dan was her big brother and a karate champion.

"I wish *I* knew karate," said Robert.

"You're not allowed to use it for fighting people you don't like," said Jemima.

"I would, though," said Robert. "Only I don't know how to do it."

"You should come to the class," said Jemima.

They were getting near the park gates and Robert's old house. "Which tree is it?" Jemima asked.

Robert pointed vaguely. "Over there."

"Can I come and see it?"

"Tomorrow," said Robert. "You'd better not keep Dan waiting."

"He's not here yet. I could come now."

Robert sighed. He might as well show her. All the kids'd be bound to come and look sooner or later. And at least she hadn't teased him. He took her to the bottom of the tree and looked up. There

44

was no sign of George or Albinia. They shinned up the trunk.

"It's quite nice for a treehouse," said Jemima as they stood on the platform, "but not for a *real* house."

"I know. That's what I keep telling them. But they won't listen."

"What about your mum?"

"She likes it too."

"They must be a bit crazy," said Jemima.

"They are," said Robert. "My dad's even stopped working."

"Have you got a biscuit?" asked Jemima.

Robert hunted around, found a packet and gave them two each.

Jemima pulled on the rope holding the bucket. "That's good," she said.

"Yes," said Robert, "but we don't use it much. They won't deliver milk or papers to us any more."

Jemima looked thoughtful. She dropped the rope and the bucket clanged as it landed on the ground. "What are you going to do?" she said.

"I don't know," said Robert miserably.

Jemima looked through the branches. "I can see Dan," she said. "He's over there by the gates. I'd better go. 'Bye." She slid down the trunk, then looked back up. "D'you want me to try and help you think of something?"

"Yes, *please*," said Robert. "'Bye."

" 'Bye." And she ran off. Robert waved through the branches.

It felt a bit lonely when she'd gone. He looked round for a note from George or Albinia but there wasn't one. Robert remembered how he and Albinia used to have tea in their real house after school and he felt a lump in his throat. Quickly, he got his football, slid down the trunk and went off to the other side of the park to practise. After a while, it started to drizzle. The biscuit hadn't been very filling and Robert was looking forward to some proper food. He picked up the ball, brushed the loose mud off himself and plodded back across the park. As he got to the base of the tree, he sniffed but there was no delicious dinner smell drifting down to him. Robert's heart sank a bit. "Mum!" he called.

Albinia's head poked through the branches. "Ssh!" she whispered and put a finger to her lips.

"What is it?" asked Robert.

"Your father's thinking. You mustn't disturb him."

"Thinking?" Robert was puzzled.

George's head popped out beside Albinia's. "Really!" he said crossly. "How can I possibly compose if people are shouting and screaming underneath my house?"

"Not people, dear. It's Robert," said Albinia. "And he didn't know you were composing."

"Just go away for half an hour, Robert," said George. "I'm in the clutches of the Muse." He held his head dramatically.

Robert, who had no idea what he meant, stood his ground. "I don't *want* to go away. I'm hungry."

Albinia came slithering down the rope ladder. She had the biscuit packet in her hands. She smiled at Robert and kissed him. "Here, have some biscuits," she said. "George won't be long. He's just working out a difficult rhyme in his poem."

"His *poem?*" said Robert.

"Yes, dear. He's decided to write poetry now he's living close to Nature. He used to be very good at it. He once sent me a lovely Valentine's Day verse."

"I don't want biscuits," said Robert. "I need dinner."

"Oh, dinner," said Albinia. "Yes, well, of course we will have dinner but not for a little while."

"We always have dinner at six o'clock," said Robert.

"We always *used to*, in the old boring life," said Albinia, "but now, with our new adventurous life, we eat when we're hungry, as Nature intended."

"I am hungry," said Robert.

"Yes, dear, I know. I told you to have a biscuit."

Robert threw down his ball and stamped off towards the pond. Albinia went back up the tree.

"Robert seems very upset about something," she said to George.

"No spirit of adventure," grunted George. "Would you say 'shadow' rhymes with 'meadow'."

"I think so, dear," said Albinia doubtfully.

11

Robert woke up early next morning, very hungry. Albinia and George were up already. It was drizzling again. "It'll clear soon," said George. "Shall I read you another poem before breakfast?"

"What *is* for breakfast?" asked Robert.

"There's a tiny bit of muesli, and milk, and some prunes," said Albinia.

"I want proper breakfast. I'm hungry," said Robert.

"You can't be. Not after that great big supper you had," said George.

"Cold tinned macaroni and gooseberries don't fill you up," said Robert in a bitter voice.

"Never mind," said Albinia, "soon we'll be eating only our own food: everything we've picked or gathered or caught. Nothing bought in a shop." She smiled at Robert. "You've got a special treat this morning. While we have breakfast, George is going to read his poems to us."

Albinia and Robert sat down and George rose to his feet.

"Don't slurp your milk, Robert," he said. "It spoils the effect."

He cleared his throat and began.

" 'Thoughts' by George Parker.

Art and Nature joined together.
We love our tree dwelling
Whatever the weather."

"That's *beautiful*, George," said Albinia. "Isn't it, Robert?"

"More milk, please," said Robert.

"Oh dear, we seem to be out of it," said Albinia. "Go on, George."

George looked pleased. He cleared his throat again.

" 'How Beautiful' By George Parker.

How beautiful to sit upon the bough
Here and now,
And see the little birdies peeking through
Looking at me and you
And Robert, too.

Verse Two

How beautiful to live in Nature's arms,
Amidst her charms.
How very, very foolish we would be,
To leave this tree,
We happy three."

"That's dedicated to you," he said to Albinia. She blushed. "You are romantic," she said softly.

"Happy three," said Robert. "*I'm* not happy. I *hate* it here."

"Robert!" cried Albinia. "That's disloyal! And after all we've done for you!"

"I should think you'd be pleased to have a father who's a poet," said George. "I don't understand you,

Robert, really I don't. I was thinking of offering to come and read my poems to your class at school but I certainly won't now."

Beads of sweat stood out on Robert's forehead. His father in school reading that terrible poetry. Things were getting worse. He sat still without saying anything.

"I think you'd better be going off to school," said Albinia. "You can have school dinner today, if you like."

"No!" cried Robert. School dinner meant having to sit with Dennis and Andy and Dominic and everyone teasing him.

"There's nothing left in the tins," explained Albinia.

Robert thought wildly. "If you give me a note for Mr Keen," he said, "I can have lunch at Jemima's. She asked me yesterday."

"I thought you didn't like Jemima," said Albinia.

"I do now," said Robert. "I . . . she . . . I want to talk to her brother about karate."

"Not fighting," reproved Albinia.

"Karate's an art form, Albinia," said George. "From the mysterious East."

Albinia wrote the note and Robert set off for school.

12

He had to endure more teasing when he went in the gate but as they lined up to go into the classroom he managed to whisper to Jemima that he wanted to have lunch at her house. She nodded. "I'll meet you just outside the gates," she hissed back.

Mr Keen must have heard about the Parkers' change of house because he said quite kindly to Robert, "How're you enjoying the outdoor life?" Robert shuffled his feet. "It's all right," he muttered.

"Well, let me know if you've got any problems," offered Mr Keen.

"I'd like to," thought Robert desperately, "but what could he do anyway?"

"Yes, sir," he said aloud.

At lunchtime, he raced out of the building and waited outside the gate for Jemima.

"What about your mum?" he asked as she came up to him. "Won't she mind?"

"She's at work," said Jemima. "But my great-aunt's at home. She won't mind. What d'you want to eat?"

'*Hot* baked beans on toast," said Robert eagerly. "And beefburgers, if you've got any."

"We've got loads," said Jemima. "We always have lots of food. There's eight of us counting Mum and Dad and Birdie."

"Who's Birdie?"

"My great-aunt. She's called that because she won two thousand pounds in a flying competition."

"Gosh," said Robert. "What did she do with all the money?"

"Bought a motorbike and some bagpipes and took some lessons," said Jemima. "She practises every day. It's awful."

"My dad's started to learn the flute. That's awful too," said Robert. "Only he isn't taking any lessons. He says he's 'one of Nature's pupils'."

"What's that mean?"

"I dunno. I think he's gone a bit barmy. They both have," said Robert.

Jemima nodded. "Have you noticed how many grown-up people *are* barmy?" she said. They were turning in at her gate. There was a motorbike resting in the side garden, and an old pushchair, and a dog kennel but no dog. Jemima pushed open the back door. "Robert's come for lunch," she announced.

A tall angular lady rose from the sofa in the corner. "You're early today," she said in a broad Scots accent.

"Can we have beefburgers, Birdie? Please. And beans on toast."

"Och, aye," said Birdie. "Why not take Robert and wash your hands now?"

Robert listened to her, fascinated. She rolled all her "r's".

"And where do you live, Robert?" she asked.

Robert went red. "Ah . . . I . . . we . . ." he began.

"He used to live at 11 Park Drive but they've moved," broke in Jemima.

Birdie looked hard at him. "Eleven Parrrk Drrive," she repeated thoughtfully. "But that's Mrs Williams's daughter's house. The one whose husband's gone mad and taken his family to live up a tree."

"We'll just go and wash our hands," said Jemima quickly. "Come on, Robert."

"Is George Parker yer father, then?" asked Birdie.

"Yes," said Robert looking at his shoes.

"Ye puir bairn," said Birdie. "I'll put an egg on yer beefburger, shall I? Take him up now Jemima, there's a good wee lass."

13

Birdie had cooked a huge amount of lunch. She piled up Robert's plate and watched him wolf it down.

"He hates living up a tree," confided Jemima. "He wants to get his mum and dad to go back home but they won't."

"I can't even call them Mum and Dad any more," said Robert with his mouth full. "I'm not allowed. I have to call them Albinia and George."

Birdie shook her head. "Yer grandma told me," she said, shaking her head. "Mebbee yer daddy's gone a bit crazy. That's what yer grandma thinks."

"She think's it's *my* fault," burst out Robert. "She thinks I made them do it."

"I'll speak to yer granny when I see her tomorrow," said Birdie, "but it sounds to me like high time to pay a wee visit to yer granny by yerself."

"Can you think of something to help Robert?" asked Jemima.

"I can try," said Birdie. "I'll have a wee play on the bagpipes now while ye and Robert do the washing-up."

"Oh, Birdie," said Jemima. "Not inside."

"Och, stop yer complaining, now," said Birdie and she picked up the bagpipes from behind the sofa. A plaintive droning sound reverberated round the kitchen. Robert watched mesmerized as Birdie squeezed the bag under her elbow then started blowing on the pipes.

"It's loud, isn't it?" he whispered to Jemima picking up a teatowel.

"Awful," she whispered back. "I really like Birdie but I can't stand her bagpipes. She usually practises outside though. Here, I've done this plate."

She passed him a plate to dry, and, as she did so, a thought struck her. "I've just had a *brilliant* idea," she announced. "Absolutely brilliant."

Birdie put the pipes down. "Ye'd better be telling us, then."

"Well," said Jemima, "it won't work on its own. Robert'll still have to find some other way of getting his parents out of the tree. But it's bound to help. Now this is what it is . . ."

14

Robert went home feeling much better. Jemima's idea was a very good one and on Saturday he would go and have a talk with Grandmother Williams. Everyone at school had teased him a lot but if he could get his parents back home it wouldn't last too long. His spirits rose. "Albinia!" he called up the tree.

George's head appeared through the foliage. "Hullo, Robert. Did you have a nice day?"

"I had a good lunch," said Robert. "Beefburgers and eggs and baked beans on toast and . . ."

Just for a moment, George looked extremely hungry and quite envious. "Not very healthy," he said. "Not like the food here."

"Cold macaroni?" asked Robert.

"No, fish," said George. "Albinia's away fishing now. I would have been bird-watching myself, but I had my flute practice and a new poem to finish."

"Uh huh," said Robert. He began to climb up the trunk.

"You might like to hear my new flute piece," said George hopefully.

"Maybe after supper," said Robert. "We could kick a ball together now, Dad, George I mean, if

61

you want."

"It's a nice idea," said George, "but the truth is I'm not feeling terribly well today."

"Are you hungry?" asked Robert.

"Of course not," said George. "It's just the poisons and toxins from the old lifestyle draining away. Albinia feels exactly the same."

"I can see Albinia's bowler hat over there," said Robert.

George looked through the branches. "Did you catch any fish?" he called down.

Albinia looked up at them sadly. "Three," she said.

"Three! That's wonderful!" shouted George enthusiastically. "Where are they?"

"Here," said Albinia holding them up for inspection.

"But they're only tiny. We can't eat *those*," cried George.

"I know," said Albinia miserably. "It'll have to be sardines again. I am sorry."

"Sardines," said George in dismay. "But we've only got one tin."

"There's some macaroni left," said Albinia and she climbed slowly up to the platform.

"Oh," said George.

"At lunchtime," said Robert, "I had beefburgers and eggs and . . ."

"Be *quiet*, Robert," snapped George. Robert smiled secretly to himself.

"Where did you actually get the fish?" he asked his mother.

"She got them in the lake, of course," said George.

"It's a pond, not a lake," said Robert. "That's why the fish are only small ones. I'll bet you're not supposed to fish in there."

Albinia looked worried. "I'm sure it's all right. There aren't any notices forbidding it," she said.

"Of course it's all right," said George, "and I wish you'd sort out supper, Albinia, instead of listening to Robert glooming on."

Albinia was annoyed. "I don't see what's to stop you doing something about supper yourself," she said coldly. "You don't seem to have done much towards the hunting and gathering of the food."

"You don't seem to realize the shortage of available birds," said George. "I suppose they sense the presence of a hunter around and make themselves scarce."

There was rustling in the branches. Robert looked up. "There's a pigeon over there," he said.

"Where?" said George.

"Right near the top of the tree," said Robert. "It's been there ages. I think it's making a nest."

"Get the binoculars!" cried his father. "Quickly!! They're over there. I'll keep watch on . . . OW!!" He clutched his left eye and hopped up and down.

"Get a handkerchief! Quick!" he shouted. "I might

be blinded for life. And stop laughing! It's not funny."

Robert and Albinia were giggling helplessly. "It's only bird-dropping," said Robert through his laughter. "It won't hurt you."

"Disgusting," said George. "That wretched bird did it on purpose."

"It's a good shot," said Robert. "I wish it was in our football team."

"Really," spluttered his father, still wiping his eye.

Robert smiled to himself. Living up a tree had some compensations after all.

15

Next morning they were woken by a dreadful commotion. A wailing, howling sound filtered through the dawn air with long slow notes shrilling over the top of it. Robert sat bolt upright nearly falling out of the hammock. He peered out of the branches. There, below the tree, stood Birdie practising her bagpipes. For a split second she winked at Robert then carried on.

Albinia's head pushed through the leaves. "Do you have any idea what time it is?" she cried furiously. "It's five o'clock in the morning!"

Birdie took no notice and went on playing. George's enraged head appeared beside Albinia's. "Go home at once!" he bellowed. "And come back at a less ungodly hour."

"Och, indeed I will not," called Birdie, stopping her piping for a minute. "I've a right to practise here whenever I choose."

"But we live here! You're interrupting our sleep," shouted Albinia.

"I don't come under your window, piping and wailing," said George crossly.

"And I dinna choose to live up a tree," retorted

Birdie, "If ye're so crazed ye wish to live like mon-keys, I'll no be stopping ye. That's yer own affair. I live in ma ain hoose and I ha' the rights ta ma ain garden but ye live in a public park and I am a member of the public. I can come here whenever I want; ye canna complain about ma practising. And I'll have ye know 'tis niver 'wailing' I'm doing. 'Tis pure Art." And she went on with her bag-piping.

"The woman's crazed," said George. "How long do you think she'll go on with it?"

"She's the aunt of a girl at my school," said Robert. "She says her aunt practises for an hour twice a week."

"An hour!" snorted George. "We may as well get up and start the day now."

"When there's a big competition she practises every day," went on Robert. Albinia put her head in her hands.

"We'd better pray there's no big competitions coming up," said George grimly.

"Well, there's nothing we can do about it if she does play," said Albinia. "She's got every right to come into the park whenever she wants."

"Of course she hasn't," said George. "What ridicu-lous nonsense. I can see the park-keeper over there. I'm going to lay a formal complaint."

"I don't think that's wise," said Albinia.

"It's my right as a treeholder," said George importantly as he clambered down the ladder. He paused beside Birdie who gave a particularly deafening blast of her pipes. "I'm afraid you leave me no alternative but to have you forcibly removed by the park authorities," he announced.

Birdie lowered her bagpipes. "Gae right ahead," she said. " 'Tis on yer ain head."

The park-keeper came striding up. "What's all this about?" he demanded.

"This woman," said George accusingly, "is disturbing the peace and I must insist that you force her to leave the park at once."

The park-keeper drew himself up. "Disturbing what peace?" he asked. "There's been no peace in this park since you arrived."

"She has no right to play that hideous instrument under my home," said George.

"I've got ivery right!" said Birdie triumphantly.

The park-keeper looked triumphantly at George. "This is a public park," he declared, "and as such is open at all specified times to any member of the public who may wish to pursue leisure activities therein. Rule 53: Section 8: Park Regulations. And if you choose to make your home up one of my trees, you'll just have to put up with it."

"You can't possibly call playing the bagpipes a leisure activity," protested George. "This woman's a public nuisance."

"Just because you don't appreciate music," said the park-keeper, "you can't expect me to stop this lady from playing. She's quite right. She's got every right to be here." He turned to Birdie. "Carry on, madam," he said graciously. "Practise wherever and whenever you choose anywhere in the park. It's a pleasure to hear you." He looked at George. "And if you have any problems with this man here, just let me know, madam."

"As a matter of fact," said George through clenched teeth, "I'm a musician myself and I am particularly fond of music. I just don't happen to like the bagpipes at any time and especially not in the early morning when I am trying to SLEEP!"

"Should have thought of that before you moved up a tree, shouldn't you!" said the park-keeper, walking off. "Good morning, madam."

Birdie picked up her pipes and began to blow again. George climbed angrily back up the ladder. "It's outrageous," he spluttered. "Absolutely monstrous! I shall complain to the council."

"You can't," said Albinia wearily. "I told you, George, there's nothing to stop her. We'll just have to make the best of it. I may as well start fishing."

"Here's your fishing rod," said George.

Albinia pulled on her clothes, ate a piece of dry bread and put on the bowler hat. She kissed Robert and George goodbye and set off for the pond carrying

her rod and folding stool.

"I don't think Albinia's very happy, George," said Robert loudly over the continuing sound of the pipes.

"Nonsense," said George. "She loves fishing every day. It's very healthy. Much better than housework."

"But she's only caught those three fish and they were too small to eat," pointed out Robert.

"She'll get better at it," said George. The bagpipes below gave a deafening blast. George slung his binoculars round his neck and kissed Robert. "I may as well get off bird-watching," he said. "Have a good day at school."

"Okay," said Robert and he waved as his father slid down the trunk, glowered at Birdie and set off across the park.

When George and Albinia were safely out of ear-shot, Birdie stopped playing and called up to Robert. He slid down the trunk.

"Puir bairn," said Birdie. "I've brought ye a bit of oatcake and bacon. D'ye think it worked?"

"It was *brilliant*," said Robert. "Really good. And I'm going to see Grandmother Williams on Saturday."

"Can ye nay go earlier?"

"No," said Robert, "or they might find out. Saturday's safer."

"Well, I'll be off now," said Birdie, "and good luck to ye."

"Will you come again?"

"In two or three days," said Birdie. "Just long enough for them to think I'm not coming." She giggled to herself and went off.

" 'Bye," called Robert. He decided to explore the park before school and try to find something for the Nature table. As he wandered towards the playground, he noticed small white mounds in the grass. He picked one. They were mushrooms. He checked underneath to make sure they weren't toadstools, then picked two more and headed off for the pond.

"Albinia!" he shouted.

"Ssh, dear," said Albinia as he puffed up. "You'll scare the fish."

"Look," said Robert. "Mushrooms."

Albinia put down her rod. "They are," she said delightedly.

"There's loads over there," said Robert.

When they had picked every single mushroom, they went back up the tree and got the pan. Robert made a fire out of small sticks and they fried the mushrooms for breakfast. Albinia smiled at him with her mouth full. "You *are* clever," she said. "That was delicious."

"Shall we save some for George?" asked Robert.

"There's hardly any left, really," said Albinia. "They'll probably be dried up completely by the time he gets back. I'll just finish them off now instead. There's bound to be some more tomorrow."

"Mum," said Robert, "didn't you like it better in our old house?"

"In a way, dear," said his mother, "but George is right. This new life is very good for us."

"It's not good for me," said Robert. "I'm cold and hungry half the time."

"The air's fresh," said Albinia.

"Not that fresh. There's cars going by the park all the time, just like our old house. And George goes birdwatching every day but he's never caught anything yet."

"It takes time," said Albinia loyally. "I'm sure he will soon."

And that very night, he did.

16

Robert had had another horrible day. He'd bumped into a gang of older boys on the way to school and they'd all started doing monkey imitations. Then, at school, Andy started teasing him about Jemima and said he ought to go and play with the girls, then Mr Keen said his homework was a mess and Robert couldn't explain it was because he'd had to do it by candlelight. And when he'd opened the lunch Albinia had packed for him, inside was a sardine and cold macaroni sandwich made with stale bread, a digestive biscuit and a handful of prunes. And, worst of all, Albinia hadn't had time to sort out their washing yet so his football kit was dirty and Mr Keen had benched him for the match.

Robert felt thoroughly fed up and disgruntled as he slouched home. There wouldn't be any dinner on when he got back and if it was sardines or cold macaroni again, he wasn't even going to eat it. He turned in at the park gates and stomped over to the pond where Albinia was fishing.

"You know what happened to me today," he began accusingly . . .

Albinia looked up. "Wonderful news, dear!" she cried, hugging him.

"We're moving back home!" said Robert.

"No, better than that! George has finally caught a pigeon!"

17

Robert looked blank. "A pigeon?"

"For supper," explained his mother. "For all of us."

"*One* pigeon for *three* people," said Robert ungraciously. "Anyway, I don't ever eat pigeon."

"Pigeon's *delicious*," said Albinia. "And this one's just the start. George says now he's got the knack of it, we'll have pigeon as often as we like."

"Cooked or raw?" asked Robert.

"Cooked, of course," said his mother.

She picked up her rod and stool and they went back to the tree together. George was standing triumphantly on the platform holding the pigeon flapping and squawking under his arm.

"I've told Robert," announced Albinia, "and he's absolutely thrilled and so proud of you. Aren't you, dear?"

Robert said nothing.

"Just like me," said Albinia and she kissed George. Robert looked away.

"Well," said George, "I finally caught it. And this was really a tough one, I can tell you."

"Tell Robert how you did it," said Albinia.

"It's all right," said Robert. "I don't mind not hearing." He turned to his mother. "I had a big problem at school today," he went on. "Mr Keen . . ."

"It was like this," interrupted George. "There was this enormous, juicy, plump pigeon roosting on a low branch when I suddenly spied it. I froze instantly – 'For Albinia's sake, and Robert's,' I said to myself, 'I mustn't fail now.' "

Albinia looked at George admiringly. George went on. "I slipped up behind it, raised my hand slowly and cautiously, then, suddenly, I STRUCK! I seized it with one mighty movement and grabbed it by the leg." He paused. The pigeon let out a sad squawk. "And now," said George grandly, "we shall eat it!" And he went to pass it to Albinia.

"But it's alive," she said in dismay.

"Of course it's *alive*," said George. "Real pigeons always are. They don't lie about plucked with their legs tied together waiting for people to pick them up and cook them."

"Who's going to kill it and pluck it, then?" asked Albinia.

"Not me," said Robert.

"Nor me," said Albinia.

" 'I will,' said the little red hen and she did'," said George. "Pass me the carving knife, Albinia."

"You can't do it with a carving knife," said Albinia.

"Of course I can."

"You can't," said Robert. "You have to wring its neck. They told us at Scouts."

"All right," said George, annoyed. "I'll wring its wretched neck then."

He put the pigeon down for a moment to get a better grip on it. Immediately it flew off, clucking and screeching, to the next branch just out of reach. George made a lunge for it, missed, and fell crashing through the branches.

"Are you all right?" screamed Albinia.

The park-keeper strode up. "How dare you chase the park pigeons! I'll have the law on you," he threatened.

George looked up. "I am NOT chasing park pigeons," he spluttered. "I am merely shooing a bird

out of my home and I'll thank you to leave me alone and stop bothering me."

The park-keeper walked off muttering. George got to his feet and started in pursuit of the pigeon which had flown to the ground and was strutting a few yards away.

"You'll never be able to kill that pigeon, Dad," said Robert. "Look at the way it's looking at you."

"My name's George," said George coldly, "and if you're trying to imply that your own father's too soft to kill a pigeon . . ."

He broke off as the pigeon waddled back towards him. "Come on! Come down and help me!" he shouted, making another wild dive at the bird. The pigeon looked disdainfully at George, shook its wings, rose into the air and flapped away out of sight.

"Goodbye, supper," said Robert from the platform.

"Ssh!" said Albinia warningly. And as George came back up the ladder, she said, "We'll just have to have sardines again, that's all."

"We can't," said George. "We've used them all up."

There was a long silence then Albinia said, "What about an omelette?"

"Wonderful!" said George.

"We haven't got any eggs," said Robert.

"Then we'll just have to borrow some," snapped George. "Pop off now to Mrs Dix, Robert, and ask her to lend your mother six eggs."

'I hate going borrowing," said Robert. "Why don't *you* go?"

"I've been out all day hunting for this family," exploded George, "and it doesn't seem too much to ask a healthy eleven-year-old boy to do his share. Off you go at once!"

"Just this once I will," said Robert. "But I'm not going to go to the Dix's. I'll go and ask Grandmother Williams."

Albinia glanced sternly at George. "That's a good idea," she said. "Go right away, there's a good boy. And be as quick as you can."

"She's weakening," thought Robert, noticing the glance. "She's getting fed up." And aloud he said, "Okay. But it might take a while to get there and back."

"Well hurry up and get started," said George testily. "Some of us are HUNGRY."

18

Robert was rather cold by the time he arrived at Grandmother Williams' house so she sat him by the fire to thaw out. "I expect you've had your supper," she said.

"No," said Robert, "I haven't. That's why I need

the eggs. We never have proper meals now."

"I'm sorry I blamed you for the move to the tree," said his grandmother. "It's not your fault at all. Birdie told me it was entirely George's idea. It's ridiculous. A man of his age."

"He's given up his job," said Robert, and he told her about the pigeon and Albinia's fishing.

"Why don't you have a bit of supper with me?" she suggested.

"Yes, please!" said Robert. She put soup and pie and potatoes and salad and ice-cream down in front of him. He wolfed it all down and warmed himself by the fire. Then he told her about the football kit.

"How *dreadful* for you," she said sympathetically. "You bring it round here tomorrow and pop it in my washing machine. What on earth's Albinia thinking of?"

"She's gone all soppy about his poetry," said Robert.

Grandmother Williams made a disapproving face. "I'm frankly amazed at Albinia," she said. "My own daughter. I thought she had more sense."

"She keeps talking about being loyal all the time," said Robert, "but I think she misses home, and proper food, too."

"Maybe you and she can join forces and get George to come to his senses," suggested his grandmother.

"I've tried," explained Robert, "but it doesn't work."

"Why don't you just come and live here with me?" asked Grandmother Williams.

Robert sighed. "They're hopeless," he said. "I've had to untangle them from their hammock, and sort out the waterproof cover, and help Albinia find the tin-opener and I even had to show them which branch to build on. They can't manage on their own."

"About time they learnt to," said his grandmother. "Selfish things. George is making a laughing stock of himself."

"They say at school, my dad's a monkey," said Robert.

"No wonder," said Grandmother Williams. "I'm starting to think so myself. How do you wash?"

"We've got a cold water hose going into the bath and we just pull the plug out when we've finished. The water falls on the ground underneath. George says it's ecological. He says it waters the grass."

"Ecological! A cold water hose! In this weather! It's outrageous!"

Grandmother Williams drew herself up. "You and I are the only sane members of this ridiculous family. We shall have to think of a plan."

"I had a sort of plan already," said Robert. "Jemima's been helping me. She's got Birdie to help, too, and she's coming to play her bagpipes again soon. But

I have to do something more than that. Jemima and I thought of a plan that might work but we need you to help as well."

"You can count on me," promised his grandmother. "What do I have to do?"

"It's like this . . ." began Robert.

19

It was very late by the time Robert got back to the tree. His grandmother walked to the park gates with him. "Come to breakfast early tomorrow," she said, "and we'll get started on the rest of the plan. Now, don't forget what you have to do."

"I won't," promised Robert. "And thank you for the supper."

"It's a pleasure," she said. "I'll be off now. We don't want George or Albinia seeing us together."

"Is that you, Robert?" called Albinia anxiously as he began to climb the ladder.

"Where have you been? We've been worried," said George. "Did you get the eggs?"

"Here," said Robert. He reached across to pass them to his father, and as he did so, he allowed his hand to slip and let the eggs smash onto the platform. "Oops!" cried Robert. "Help! Sorry! Oh gosh, it looks as if they're all broken." Albinia began to cry.

"The branch brushed my face," explained Robert untruthfully.

"We've got nothing to eat now," wept Albinia.

Robert didn't like seeing his mother cry but he

thought about his plan and said nothing.

"I'm really cross with you," snapped George glaring at Robert. "Of all the stupid . . ."

And then something extraordinary happened. Albinia stopped crying and began to get annoyed. "How dare you tell Robert off!" she cried. "Sending him out like that in the dark. You should be ashamed of yourself, George Parker!" And she flounced off to the hammock.

George looked stunned. "*Now* see what you've done," he said to Robert. "You'll just have to go without supper tonight."

Robert smiled kindly at his father. "It's all right," he said, "don't worry about me. I had mine with Grandmother Williams. We had hot soup and pie and lovely potatoes and . . ."

"Be *quiet*," said George. "And go to bed at once!"

Robert went off meekly, got into his pyjamas, and slipped into his hammock. He was smiling to himself as he fell asleep.

20

Promptly at six next morning, they were woken by the skirl of Birdie's bagpipes. "Oh *no!*" groaned George from under the blankets. And Robert heard Albinia say through clenched teeth, "I've just about had enough."

He yawned, got up and got dressed, waving secretly to Birdie. His parents were both sitting huddled on the platform looking dreadful. Albinia shivered miserably over her cup of tea. "Would you like me to play you my new flute piece?" asked George.

"*No!*" said Albinia shortly.

"I need a pee," said Robert, "but the park toilet's still locked."

"Just do it through the branches onto the ground. It won't hurt for once," said George.

"I can't with that lady down there. I might wet her," pointed out Robert.

"Good thing, too," muttered George.

"Really!" said Albinia. "Just climb down and go behind a bush."

"Someone might see," objected Robert.

Albinia considered. "You'll simply have to pop over and use the loo in our old house."

"Albinia," George was shocked and hurt. "We AGREED we wouldn't go back to the old house except in an emergency."

"This *is* an emergency," said Robert. "If I have to wait much longer, I'll wet myself."

"Here," said Albinia, "take the key and make sure you lock up afterwards."

It was eerie in his old house. It seemed very empty without anyone living in it and it smelt a bit sad and damp. He looked into his bedroom and sighed. All his posters and his Space Wars duvet-cover and his computer were still there. Even his dressing gown hung waiting on the back of the door. "I'll be back soon," he promised the empty room and went off to the tree, stopping on the way in the kitchen to collect something he had just thought of from the cupboard. Birdie was still playing as he climbed the ladder and she winked at him.

"Here's the key back," he said to Albinia.

"How's the house?"

"Fine," said Robert. "Just comfortable and ordinary. It's warm, too."

"Oh," said Albinia.

"I brought you this," said Robert, holding up a tin. "I got it from the kitchen cupboard."

George and Albinia leaned forward eagerly. "How thoughtful of you," said Albinia. "What is it, dear?"

Robert forced himself to keep a straight face. "Tapioca," he said innocently. "I thought you might like it for breakfast."

"Tapioca?" snorted George. "For breakfast?"

Albinia shot George a warning look. "That's a very nice thought, Robert," she said, "but I think, if you don't mind, I'll keep it for supper. Shall we go and try to find some mushrooms together?"

"I can't," said Robert. "I promised Mr Keen I'd get a stick insect for the Nature table so I have to go in a minute."

Birdie gave a particularly loud blast on the bagpipes and George put his hands over his ears.

"What about your breakfast?" asked his mother.

"I had such a delicious big supper last night," said Robert cheerfully, "that I don't think I'll need breakfast this morning."

He collected his school things, kissed George and Albinia and started to shin down the trunk. "Good luck with the mushroom hunting," he called. He set off whistling, picked up a stick insect and made his way to his grandmother's house.

She had a huge breakfast set out waiting for him. "And a decent packed lunch," she said. "Those two! Idiots, both of them."

"I think it's starting to work," said Robert through a mouth full of sausage and egg. "I think Mum doesn't like it so much any more. She's starting to get hungry."

"What about your father?"

"Dad'd never admit he was wrong," said Robert.

Grandmother Williams shrugged. "I'll make that phone-call to the newspaper office later on," she said.

Robert grinned at her.

"By the way, I was thinking about the teasing,"

she said.

"What?"

"At school. When they tease you, try to take no notice. It's hard, I know, but the less you react, the sooner they'll give it up."

"That's what Jemima said."

"She's right," said his grandmother. "Take no notice and next week they'll be onto something else."

"It's half term at the end of next week," said Robert. "D'you think we'll have got them back home by then?"

"Lord, yes. I wouldn't give them longer than three or four days myself."

"I hope you're right," said Robert feelingly.

21

He walked home with Jemima after school.

"Jemima's your girlfriend," called Dennis.

"You're really boring, Dennis," said Jemima. "Didn't anyone ever tell you that before?"

"The apeman's in love," said Andy. "Chee, chee, chee."

Robert took no notice.

"They're so stupid," said Jemima. "I don't know why they bother. What did your grandmother say? Will she help?"

"She thinks it's a brilliant idea," said Robert. "She says she and I are the only sane ones in my family."

"Birdie says that about me and her in my family, too," said Jemima.

"Birdie's great," said Robert. "She's driving George crazy with her bagpipes."

Jemima laughed. "It's a pretty ghastly noise," she said. "Birdie says she'd have made that phone-call for you but it's too easy to trace her accent. Your father'd be suspicious if anyone told him it was a Scotswoman who rang. He'd know it was her and it might ruin the plan."

"It's okay," said Robert. "Grandmother Williams

is dying to ring up. She says she can't wait to see George get what's coming to him."

They had reached Jemima's house. "D'you want to come in and do a bit of football practice?" she asked.

Robert went in. Birdie gave them their tea. "I'll be back with the pipes tomorrow at five-thirty," she promised. "Yer daddy's nae looking too good." She grinned. "Should'na be tae long noo."

"Grandmother Williams says they won't last more than a few more days," said Robert. "If the plan works."

"I'm sure it's going to," said Jemima.

"George's started doing Chinese exercises now," sighed Robert. "So it'd better."

They went out and practised dribbling and goal-shooting for a while then Robert decided it was time to go home.

"She was going to try to ring today," he told Jemima. "So maybe it'll have started working by the time I get home."

"Hope so," said Jemima. "Let me know, anyway."

When Robert got home, he saw at once something had happened. George and Albinia were in a great state of excitement. "We're famous!" said George. "The newspaper's heard about us. They know about my poetry and my flute playing . . ."

"And my fishing," put in Albinia.

"And they want to come and interview us."

"We'll be in the papers."

"How did they hear about it?" asked Robert.

"Someone phoned this morning and told them. I don't know who. I expect someone who admired our new original lifestyle."

Robert grinned. "When are they coming?"

"Tomorrow," said George proudly. "So we have to spend the time till then making our home look nice."

"It doesn't look nice," said Robert. "It looks uncomfortable and it *is*. You'll never be able to make it look nice whatever you do."

"Robert!" cried George. "You're utterly unsupportive."

"Perhaps, it'd be better if you didn't actually speak to any of the reporters, dear," said Albinia. "But you can be photographed in the bath, if you like."

"I'm not being photographed *anywhere*," declared Robert. "It's all right for you two. You don't have to see anyone after. I have to go to school."

"Don't be ridiculous," said George. "After the interview we'll be the most famous family in the city."

"That's just what I'm afraid of," said Robert but his parents were far too excited to hear him.

Next day, before the reporters arrived, Robert took care to climb right out of sight up to the eighth branch of the tree. He found himself a comfortable spot screened by leaves and settled down to watch and listen. There were a reporter and a photographer and they did seem very interested in George and Albinia. Robert felt a bit anxious: he hoped the plan wasn't going to backfire.

George told the reporter how ordinary his life had been before and how exciting it was to have to hunt and search for your own food.

"Do you eat well?" asked the reporter.

"Magnificently," replied George. "And very healthily, as well."

Robert thought of the cold macaroni and sardines. "If *I* told lies like that, there'd be trouble," he said to himself.

"And you like it better than your old way of living?" asked the reporter.

"Wouldn't go back to the old way for anything," declared George.

"And when I think of how long I used to spend on housework," put in Albinia, "I'm amazed every woman doesn't prefer to live up a tree."

The questions went on for ages. Then George offered to play his flute for them and had just started when the park-keeper came into view.

"What are you up to now?" he roared. "Encouraging tourists! Letting them trample all over my nice clean grass. You're a menace! I wish I'd never laid eyes on you! Go and squat in someone else's park!"

"The park-keeper doesn't seem too sympathetic to your new lifestyle," remarked the photographer as the keeper marched away.

"We're leaders," explained George. "And pioneers. Naturally, not everyone understands our way of life yet. He may not admit it but that park-keeper's already been softened by my poetry and flute-playing."

Albinia looked uncomfortable. "Er, why don't you read some of your poetry now?" she suggested.

George looked modest. "They may not want to hear it, Albinia," he protested.

"Always love to hear poetry, Mr Parker," said the reporter. "Fire away."

George was pleased. He recited several poems. Robert thought they were terrible but the reporter seemed impressed and the photographer took several pictures of George reading and playing and some of Albinia with her fishing rod.

"What about a family picture with your little boy?" he asked.

Robert shot him an unseen withering look through the branches. Little boy indeed! George and Albinia called and searched but they couldn't find Robert anywhere.

"Never mind," said the photographer. "We'll get a shot of you and your wife sitting on the platform together and another in the hammock and, yes, one like that, peering through the branches."

After a while it was all over and they trooped away. Robert waited till his parents went off for a walk then he climbed down and lay in his hammock.

"You missed it all, Robert. What a pity," said Albinia when they returned.

"It would have been nice for you to have had your picture in the papers," said George.

"No, it wouldn't," said Robert. "Not unless it

was in the football team or rescuing people from a fire or something."

"You are a funny boy," said his mother.

Robert snorted.

22

Next day was Saturday. Robert got up early before George and Albinia were awake, took his pocket money and went off to meet Jemima at the corner shop. She was there already clutching the paper. "It's in!" she cried. "And it's really terrible! Look!"

She thrust the paper at him. There on the front page, with three large photographs, was the headline

"NEW AGE APE-MAN TAKES UP RESIDENCE
IN THE PARK."

"Your father will be pretty cross," said Jemima. "It makes him sound crazy."

Just for a minute, Robert felt very mean. Then he remembered the tinned macaroni and the cold baths and his new life up the tree.

"Serves him right," he said. "Let's take it round to my grandmother's and have some breakfast. We can look at it properly there."

Grandmother Williams came to the door in her nightgown. "You're early," she said.

"We've got the paper," explained Robert.

"Quickly, let me see the front page," said his grandmother. "Wonderful! Couldn't be better. Come on in and we'll all read it together over early breakfast."

"They're not going to be too pleased," said Robert. "Look at this photograph. It says underneath, 'MRS MONKEY SWINGS THROUGH HER HOUSEWORK.' Albinia will be very upset."

"That's her problem," said his grandmother. "She's the one who insisted on living up a tree."

"It was George, really," said Robert.

"Well, she should have refused to go along with it," said Grandmother Williams. "I don't know what she's thinking of."

"She's definitely getting fed up," said Robert.

"She was cross with Dad yesterday."

"About time, too," said Jemima. "Look at what it says here." She passed the paper over to Robert. He laughed.

"Thank goodness you and I aren't in it," said Grandmother Williams. "Why don't we all go to the zoo for the day and leave those two to read the paper on their own. Ring your mother, Jemima, and see if you can come."

"Shouldn't I just go and tell Mum and Dad where I'm going?" asked Robert. "They might be worried."

"Normally I'd say yes," said his grandmother, "but I really don't think it would do them any harm to worry about you for a bit. *If* they even notice you're not there."

"They'll probably be too busy looking at the paper," said Jemima, coming back from the phone.

"Very likely," said Grandmother Williams. "What did your mother say?"

"She's out," said Jemima, "but Birdie says it's fine for me to go with you, thank you."

"We can have lunch at McDonald's if you want," said Grandmother Williams.

"I love McDonald's," said Jemima.

"And me," said Robert.

"Jemima's been a real help to you," said Robert's grandmother, "and I hope you know it."

"I do!" said Robert. "Don't go on at me."

"I'm going to the panda house when we get to the zoo," said Jemima.

"I'm going to see the elephant being weighed," said Robert.

"Well, don't start arguing," said Grandmother Williams. "I'm sure there'll be time to do both. Why not get ready now?"

Robert went back to the treehouse after a very satisfactory day with his grandmother and Jemima. His grandmother had given him an early supper "just in case" and he was feeling much happier than he had for a long time. He climbed up the ladder whistling happily. There was silence from the platform. At first Robert thought no one was home, then he realized both his parents were there but were sitting coldly ignoring each other at opposite ends of the platform. "Hi!" said Robert.

Silently, Albinia held out the paper. "Read that," she said. Robert read the story again being very careful not to laugh.

"Well . . ." he began.

"How disgusting!" cried Albinia. "What a dreadful, degrading article! And look at the picture. Two savages leering out of a tree."

"But you *do* look a bit like that," said Robert. "Your hair's grown and so's George's. *And* his beard."

"That's very unkind of you," said George. "It's just an unflattering picture."

"IT IS NOT!" shouted Albinia. "You *do* look like that. I've got so used to you I hadn't noticed, but your hair's all bushy and your beard's stubbly and awful. And I used to be so proud of you."

"How disloyal!" cried George. "I'm ashamed of you."

Albinia picked up her fishing rod and broke it over her knee. "I've had enough!" she yelled. "I'm

hungry all the time and I'm cold and I WANT TO GO HOME!"

"Never in a million years!" said George firmly. "You can be feeble and boring and unexciting and go back to the old life if you want to, but *I* shall stay on with my poetry and my flute and my new life."

"You could always play the flute and write poetry in the old house," said Robert.

George ignored this. "Just don't talk to me. I'm

going to have my bath," he said grandly. "Don't disturb me, please." And he went off.

Albinia looked angrily at Robert. "What a *horrible* article," she said. "Those reporters made it all different from the way it really is."

"I think they made it sound better," said Robert. Albinia looked upset.

George was singing in his bath. He had put the words of one of his poems to the tune of "A Life on the Ocean Wave". Robert sighed.

"Where've you been all day?" asked his mother. "We had no idea what had happened to you."

"I went . . ." Robert began, but his words were

drowned in a torrent of screaming and shouting. Albinia and Robert moved to the edge of the platform and peered over. At the foot of the tree stood the park-keeper, soaking wet and furious.

"How dare you?" he spluttered. "You fool! You imbecile! You *trespasser!* I'll have you put out of that tree if it's the last thing I do. Drenching a park-keeper in the execution of his duties! I'll have the law on you!"

George was standing in the bath wrapped in a big blue bath-towel. "You are standing under my bathroom," he said grandly. "You have positioned yourself right where the water pours down the plug-hole so you have, naturally, got wet."

"*Your bathroom!*" roared the park-keeper. "What're you talking about? You're up a tree letting water fall down on innocent people's heads. And *cold* water at that."

"This tree is my home and you are standing under my bathroom waste-pipe. *I* can't be held responsible for what happens to you," said George.

"Right," said the park-keeper. "You're for it, you are." And he shook the water off his cap and strutted off.

"I think George is making a serious mistake," said Robert.

"So do I," said Albinia. But neither of them said anything to George.

23

Half an hour later Robert heard movements under the tree. He craned down and saw the park-keeper raking up leaves and papers into a large pile. "Look," he whispered to his parents. The park-keeper looked up at the tree and scowled, then lit a match and dropped it right into the middle of the pile. Smoke began to drift upwards and very soon they were all coughing and spluttering as great clouds of it floated round them.

"Serves you right!!" shouted the park-keeper from below. "Smoke out vermin, that's what you always do."

"I pay my taxes and I've got every right to live here," bellowed George.

"And I've got every right to light my fires where I choose," retorted the park-keeper and he strode away triumphantly. Up the tree, they were choking and gasping.

"We'll have to go for a walk till it dies down," said Albinia.

"It's seven o'clock," said George. "It's supper-time."

"We can't cook supper in all this smoke," said

Albinia. "Come *on*, George. Don't be so gormless."
George looked offended but he picked up his flute and
climbed down the trunk with Robert and Albinia.

Robert was in good spirits. Things were going
nicely. Tomorrow he would slip over to his grandmother's and let her know. Albinia was talking about
the newspaper article again.

"Your poems don't seem the same written down
like that," she said to George.

"They're meant to be read aloud by someone
who understands Art," said George loftily.

"Oh George, don't be silly," said Albinia. "They
ought to look just as good written down."

"You've obviously lost confidence in me," said
George.

"No," said Albinia. "Well, not a lot."

The bonfire seemed to have died down as they
went back to the tree for a light supper of digestive
biscuits and cold water. "The gas has run out again,"
explained Albinia.

"I don't mind," said Robert generously, thinking
of his earlier supper with Grandmother Williams. "I
like digestive biscuits."

George didn't say a word and Albinia looked at the
supper in distaste. "It's that or nothing, I suppose,"
she said. There was still a distinct smell of burnt
leaves and paper in the air. It was unpleasant and
made everything taste stale and sooty. They went

to bed very early – as Albinia pointed out it wasn't as if there was any television to watch and there wasn't very much they could do without any lights to see by.

"Goodnight, dear," called Albinia from their hammock.

"Goodnight," said Robert. "Oh, by the way I met that girl from school today and she told me her aunt's probably going to practise every day this week. She's going in for a competition."

"Oh NO!!!" groaned George.

"Never mind," said Robert. "It's healthy to get up early with the sun." George looked suspiciously in the direction of Robert's hammock but said nothing.

24

Robert sat bolt upright in his hammock. It was pitch dark and the whole tree seemed to be lurching and swaying. What time was it? It must be the middle of the night. There was no moon and the sky was black. He couldn't see a thing. The wind moaned and howled and the tree shook again. His hammock was bouncing around dangerously.

He decided to get out of it and sleep up on the platform and, just as he climbed to the next branch, there was an almighty CRACK!, then a crash, and branches came hurtling across his hammock. Robert shivered. Something was badly wrong. There came a clap of thunder and a flash of lightning which briefly lit up the park. The helterskelter in the playground had fallen over and the oak tree next to their tree was lying on its side, uprooted, with its branches obscuring Robert's hammock. "Thank goodness I wasn't in it!" he thought and shivered.

Splat! A fat drop of rain fell on his head, followed by another and another until it was pouring down. The plastic must have been torn away by the wind. "Robert! Are you all right!" It was his mother's voice.

"Something's wrong," said Robert. "It feels like

a hurricane. I'm up here on the platform and the plastic's blown away and there's a whole load of branches over my hammock."

He saw Albinia shine a torch. "Good Heavens!" she cried. "It's a miracle you weren't killed! Wake up, George!" She shook him.

George didn't move. "He took a pill because he was having trouble sleeping," she explained to Robert.

Robert looked at George in disgust as the torch shone on him. All that talk about the outdoor life being healthy and here he was having to take pills to sleep. Another great spasm shook the tree. "Mum," said Robert firmly, "I've had enough. I'm not living up this tree any longer. It's crazy and I'm wet and cold. You and Dad can stay up here as long as you like but I'm going home. Give me the key, please."

Albinia fished around inside the teapot and pulled out the key. "I'll come over with you," she said. She looked anxiously at the hammock. "I only hope another tree doesn't fall on George while I'm gone."

By the time they had crossed the park and got to the gates, they were soaking wet and Robert's suitcase was dripping. Albinia put the key into the lock and let them in.

They stood in the hall making puddles on the carpet. "It looks nice, doesn't it?" said his mother. "So cosy." She took some towels and dried herself

and Robert, made him some hot cocoa and tucked him into bed.

"Mum," said Robert, "why don't you stay here, too?"

Albinia was torn. "I'd like to," she said. "I really would. But George does need me, and I shouldn't back out now. And you're supposed to call me Albinia, dear. You know that."

"*I'm* not going back," said Robert. "Never! I'm going to live here."

Albinia sighed. "Go to sleep now," she said, "and we'll discuss it tomorrow." And she blew him a kiss as she left.

25

Robert woke up to the sound of the telephone. At first he couldn't think where he was, then he remembered. He struggled out of bed and onto the landing. It was his grandmother.

"I just had a feeling the storm might have helped," she said. "I'll be over to see you later with Jemima. She came round yesterday with Birdie. She said to tell you Birdie's prepared to play every morning this week."

"That's nice of her," said Robert. "By the way, I've told Mum I'm not going back."

"You stand firm," said his grandmother. "I'll be round in an hour or so."

Robert put down the phone and went to the window. It was still raining heavily though the wind had died down. All over the park was a scene of devastation. Shrubs were smashed and broken, rubbish bins had blown over, and a section of the park railings was lying on the footpath. It must have been a hurricane in the night.

He decided to unpack then go downstairs and see what he could find to eat. Whistling happily, he pulled his things out of his suitcase and put them back on his shelves. By the time Grandmother Williams and Jemima arrived he was dressed and fed and ready.

"You two peep out the living room window and see if you can see anything," said his grandmother. "I'll start getting this pie organized."

Robert and Jemima looked out. Under the tree they could just see two figures obviously having an argument. The smaller one was waving her arms and shaking her fist.

"Well, it looks as if your mother'll be back later," said Jemima.

Robert went off to tell his grandmother. "Jemima's right," she said. "I guarantee it. You'd better get your cooking organized now so you're ready."

"D'you think she'll come straight away?" said Robert.

"This evening's my guess," said Grandmother Williams. "I'll stay the night if she doesn't come but if she does, Jemima and I will slip away out of the other door. Oh, there's a cake in the basket for you two, by the way. You can eat it while you watch television. It's far too wet to go out."

Robert and Jemima spent a nice afternoon watching television while the rain beat and drummed on the windows. It got dark quite early. "Put the light on now," said his grandmother. "Just long enough for them to notice it and see how inviting it looks. Then draw the curtains. Jemima and I'll stay out of sight."

They played computer games for a while, then Jemima went to peep out of the window again. "I can't see anything," she said. "It's pitch dark out there. But it's still pouring with rain. They must be soaked. I'm sure at least your mother'll come back."

"Dad's really stubborn," said Robert. "I don't think he'll give up very easily."

"He must be awfully stubborn to stay out in this weather," said Jemima. "Pass me some more cake, will you? It's delicious."

Robert cut her another slice.

"D'you want me to help you with the pie before I go?" she asked.

"It's all right thanks," said Robert. "You're going to get awfully wet going home, though."

"No, I won't," said Jemima. "Birdie's picking me up on her motor-bike and I'm going to wear Dan's motor-bike cape."

"I hope Mum and Dad don't see her," said Robert anxiously.

"They won't," said Jemima. "Birdie's going to cut the lights and the engine down the road."

Just at that moment they heard a knock at the door.

"Mum!" breathed Robert.

"No, Birdie," said Jemima. "She said she'd be here about now."

Grandmother Williams called up the stairs, "Jemima, it's Birdie."

They went downstairs. Birdie was standing in the kitchen in a bright yellow raincape.

"Och, I've come for Jemima," she said. "It's nae a good night ta be oot. I'm thinking ye'll get them home tonight, laddie." And she winked at Robert. "Good luck. Put Dan's cape on now, Jemima, and we'll creep away off home."

" 'Bye, Robert," said Jemima. "Good luck. 'Bye, Mrs. Williams. Thanks for the cake."

"See you tomorrow," said Robert. "Thanks for all the help. And thanks, Birdie."

"Och, it was a pleasure," said Birdie. "I'm hoping ye'll get them both to come to their senses."

"They'd better," said Grandmother Williams meaningly. " 'Bye, Birdie. And thanks. Goodbye, Jemima."

They slipped off into the pouring rain.

"And now for that pie," said Grandmother Williams. "Come on, Robert. I'll show you what to do then I'd better be ready to slide out of the front door myself."

"Maybe they won't come at all," said Robert.

"We'll just have to wait and see," said Grandmother Williams, "but at least the weather's on our side."

Half an hour later, Robert put the pie in the oven, put the potatoes on to boil and made a salad. Then he set the kitchen table for one. Outside it was still raining. There was a scuffle at the back door. Grand-mother Williams went quietly into the hall, winked at Robert and vanished. Then there came a timid knock. "Who is it?" called Robert.

"It's Mum, dear," said Albinia's voice, from the porch.

Robert unlocked the door. "Hullo, Mum," he said.

Albinia was carrying a bag with quite a lot of her things in it. "It's terribly wet and cold out there," she said.

"I know," said Robert.

"I think I'm getting a chill," said Albinia.

"You probably are," said Robert.

Albinia sniffed. "Something smells very good," she said.

"Oh, just pie and potatoes," said Robert. And he went on getting the meal ready.

"It does smell delicious," said his mother, drying her hair on the kitchen towel. "Er . . . Do you think . . . I mean . . . Could George and I have some?"

"No," said Robert, "but you and Dad could."

"Where shall I sit?" asked his mother.

"No need to sit down," said Robert cheerfully. "Go back up the tree and I'll put it in the bucket when it's ready. You can haul it up."

His mother looked embarrassed. She cleared her throat awkwardly. "The thing is," she said, "I'm not going back up the tree. I've come home. George is staying up there on his own."

Robert said nothing but he started to set another place at the table. "You can sit here," he offered. From the living room, he heard the faint sounds of his grandmother leaving. He looked at Albinia but she hadn't noticed.

"I've decided," she was saying, "that George was right when he said this family was boring, but living up a tree's not the way to change that."

"*I'm* not boring," said Robert indignantly.

His mother got up and hugged him. "No, you're not," she said. "Not a bit."

"What'll you do now?" asked Robert.

"I've decided to get a job," said Albinia. "One good thing I've found out is how boring housework is. From now on we'll have a rota and divide it up amongst all of us."

Robert drained the potatoes, put on the oven gloves and carefully took the pie out of the oven.

"Robert!" cried his mother. "How magnificent!"

Robert looked modest. "Just an ordinary pie, really," he said as he set it on the table.

"It looks absolutely delicious," said Albinia. "And

I'm starving."

They had just started to eat it when there was a noise at the back door. They looked at each other. The door opened and there, looking shamefaced, stood George.

"Hi, Dad," said Robert.

"It's a bit cold up that tree," said his father. "It's lovely and warm in here."

"That's what Mum said," said Robert.

"What's Mum eating?" asked his father.

"Oh just a bit of pie and potatoes and salad," said Robert.

"It looks wonderful," said George greedily. "I wouldn't mind a bit myself."

"I'll bring some afterwards and put it in the basket for you," offered Robert.

"The thing is," said his father, "I mean . . ." He stopped.

"Yes?" said Robert.

"I was thinking," went on his father, "that there's nothing to stop me taking flute lessons even if I don't live in a tree."

"No," said Robert through a mouthful of pie. "That's what I said the other day."

"We could go on foreign holidays," said George. "And do interesting things at home."

"I'm going to get a job," announced Albinia.

"That's a good idea," said George.

"Well," said Robert, "if you go on back up the tree, I'll bring your pie over as soon as I can."

George sighed.

"What is it, Dad?"

"It's a bit lonely up that tree."

"Yes?" said Robert.

"I think," said George, "I just might move back home. It really does seem the most sensible thing to do."

Robert set a place for George and dished out some potatoes and pie. George sat munching for a while then he said, "What a wonderful meal."

"Just an ordinary pie and potatoes," said Robert.

His father looked around. "It's a very warm, cosy kitchen, isn't it?" he said.

"Quite ordinary, really," said Robert.

"When you think about it, there's something rather nice about being ordinary," said his father.

"Comfortable," said Robert. "Like I've always said. D'you want me to give you and Mum a hand to bring the things back to the house tomorrow?"

"If you don't mind," said his father humbly.

Robert smiled. "It's all right, Dad," he said. "Now, what about another bit of pie?"

THE END